RISE UP AND WRITE IT

WRITTEN BY NANDINI AHUJA AND ILLUSTRATED BY ANOOSHA SYED

HARPER FESTIVAL
An Imprint of HarperCollinsPublishers

To Trisha, for marching, organizing, teaching, learning,
and being a sister activist

To activists around the world who want justice now
—N.A.

For Mikael
—A.S.

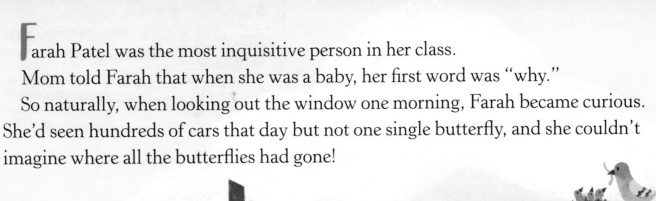

Farah Patel was the most inquisitive person in her class.

Mom told Farah that when she was a baby, her first word was "why."

So naturally, when looking out the window one morning, Farah became curious. She'd seen hundreds of cars that day but not one single butterfly, and she couldn't imagine where all the butterflies had gone!

Whenever Farah had a question she couldn't answer, she went to Mom first. Mom knew *everything*.

"Why aren't there butterflies in our neighborhood anymore?" she asked.

"They need nectar from flowers to live, and there aren't enough on our block," Mom said.

Farah couldn't help but think, "That *isn't* right."

Farah looked around her neighborhood. It was full of friendly neighbors, funny dogs, and delicious food. There just wasn't enough green.

What would YOU like to do with this public land?

Send your ideas to Mayor Khan at 39 Joy Lane and make Grove Hills the best it can be.

But then Farah spotted a big poster on the fence surrounding an empty lot, which gave her an even bigger idea.

Farah borrowed Dad's nicest stationery and Mom's fanciest fountain pen, and in her best handwriting, she wrote to Mayor Khan.

Farah knew exactly what to do with the empty lot—turn it into a beautiful community garden!

A few days later, Mayor Khan wrote back to congratulate Farah on her great idea. But she had some not so great news too.

The Dullard Gravel Company had proposed to buy the empty lot and turn it into a parking lot. Mayor Khan was sorry to say the city council was about to accept their plan.

At first, Farah was bummed. Then she realized that the plan hadn't been accepted—at least not *yet*.

Farah invited her friends over and told them about her idea.

"A community garden next door would mean more flowers, fresh fruits, and plenty of veggies," she explained.

"And cool bugs and birds," chimed in her best friend, Steven Chen.

"Absolutely," said Farah. "Who will help me get signatures for a petition to show the city council what our neighborhood *really* wants?"

Everyone raised their hands.

Pocket of Powerful Petitions!

Remember to:

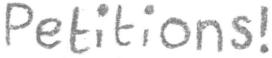

1. Know your Stuff
2. Bring a buddy
3. Never give up

Farah and her friends sharpened their pencils, ready for the journey ahead. They knocked on every door in the neighborhood and shared their big idea.

And after a week of going door-to-door and climbing up hundreds of steps, they had pages and pages of signatures.

Farah mailed Mayor Khan the petition, and a few days later, the mayor wrote back.

"Wow! It does seem like a lot of people want a
community garden in the neighborhood. We will hold a
public forum in one week to decide on the matter. I hope
to see you there."

A public forum sounded like a big deal.
Farah decided to call for backup and
organized a community meeting.

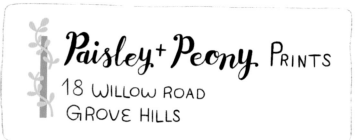

Paisley + Peony. PRINTS
18 WILLOW ROAD
GROVE HILLS

55¢

55¢

Farah Patel

12 Chester Ave

Apt. 3A

Grove Hills

Paisley + Peony Prints
18 Willow Road
Grove Hills

To prepare for the meeting, Mom packed tacos and lemonade.

"It's hard to come up with a plan on an empty stomach," she said.

As they walked to the library together, arms full of tasty treats, Farah wondered if anyone would attend. What if no one saw the posters?

But when she opened the doors, the room was full, and everyone was ready to help figure out a way to make the community garden a reality.

Everyone at the meeting spoke up. Some people shared their love of picking berries in the summer. Others said they wished they could garden in the spring. One thing was clear: their community believed that a garden would make their lives better, and a parking lot would not.

"Then we have to show the city council how we feel," said Farah.

Together, they planned a trip to city hall in support of the garden. Farah had never been prouder to live in Grove Hills.

✳ Superb Signs ✳

1. Think of a slogan

2. Use your outside voice

3. ~~Beliv~~ Believe in yourself!

One by one, Farah and her neighbors arrived at city hall.

Some people carried colorful signs with fun slogans or bright drawings. Others came up with catchy chants that got the whole crowd to join in.

Everyone was there to show their support for the community garden.

Once everyone arrived, people wanted Farah to talk. They started chanting, "Speech! Speech!"

The clerk gave Farah the microphone. She spoke about how having a community garden would help the people of Grove Hills live a happier, healthier life.

"I love my hometown," she said. "And I want to make it better."

Everyone cheered, and Mayor Khan clapped the hardest.

Seeing everyone holding signs and speaking their minds, Mayor Khan and the city council announced that they had come to their decision.

"We hear you loud and clear. Grove Hills is going to get a whole lot greener!" Mayor Khan happily proclaimed.

After weeks of writing letters, planning meetings, and taking action, the neighborhood was going to get its community garden!

Soon, everywhere she looked, Farah began to see things she could help make better. And then she noticed all the other students who wanted to make things better too.

Farah knew she wasn't done helping, so she started a club at school for kids looking to change the world.

Our First YAASP Meeting! ☺

Together, they called themselves the
"Young Activists After-School Program."

young ACTiViSTS

⇒ after-school ⇐

PROGRAM

Grove Hills Elementary School | Grove Hills

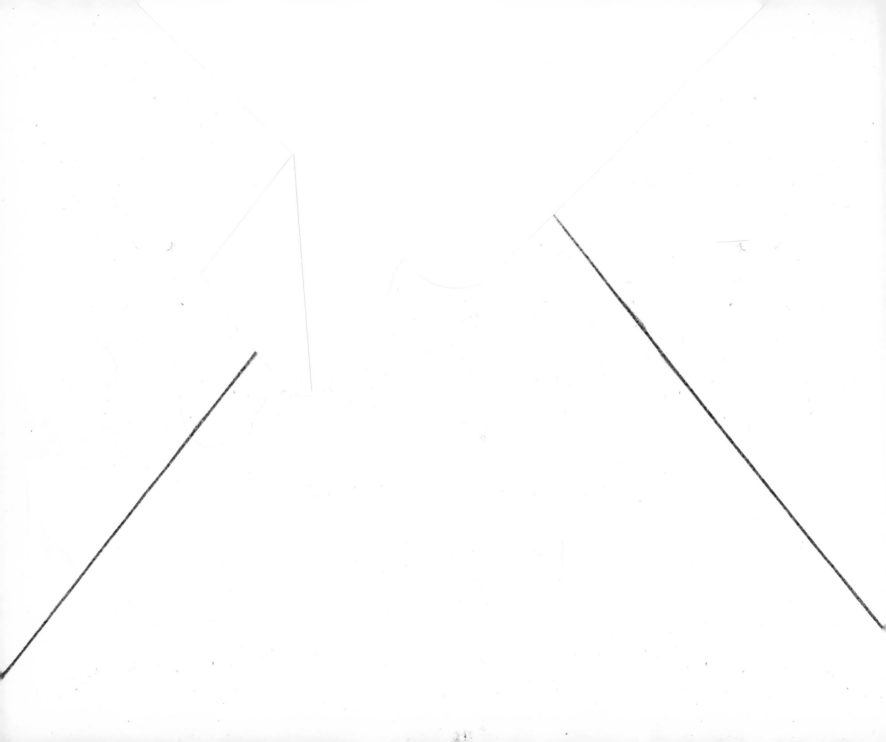

Farah and the rest of the Young Activists got the school to make healthier lunches, fix the broken swings on the playground, and start a debate team!

Even though they didn't win every fight, Farah knew they were building a better neighborhood.

Every so often, Farah wrote the mayor to give her updates on the Young Activists and all the work they were doing in the city. And when the community garden was finally ready, Farah invited her to the grand opening.

"Maybe one day we can work together at city hall," said Mayor Khan during the celebration as she admired all the plants they were growing.

When Farah wasn't with the Young Activists, she was usually at the garden with her parents, planting seeds, watering the plants, or picking fresh peppers. And if she was really lucky, she would spot a butterfly.

The fluttering butterflies that flew in the neighborhood always reminded Farah that their big, beautiful garden had started from a tiny, curious question. With hard work, tons of help, and a lot of courage, it had become a place full of life. Farah made herself a promise to never stop asking "Why?" and to always try to make the world a greener, healthier, happier place.